INVISIBLE

For Will

1.

The door slammed shut and sent a shudder from his teeth to his toes. He saw the woman peer across the top of her newspaper; a red top rag of speculation and slander, no doubt. They both sat in the cafeteria, a room dripping in squalor where the most disgusting odour wafted through the vent and spread across the air. It had once been a hive of activity during break periods and lunch hours, but the cafeteria had long since taken second place to the more inviting Cote's Bar across the street. Joe preferred the solitude of the dismal little room though, which allowed him to block out the melee and dive into his thoughts.

Louise Bradshaw had made eye contact with him first. An awkward glance had become a curious smirk, which then became an exchange of friendship. Much to his surprise, she had even entered into conversation. Until the silence had been broken, the only sound in the room had been the hum of the antiquate refrigerator. Her silence had bothered him. Not least, because it had alienated her from building friendships, or even professional relationships within the organisation. There was also the cruel jibes and silent treatment that was meted out to her by the majority of the office. Joe wasn't quite sure what she had done to upset them so much, but they avoided her like the plague. The only conclusion he had found was that her brisk demeanour had put a barrier between herself and everybody she came into contact with. Now that he was getting to know her, he wasn't quite so sure.

For a woman barely more than five foot two, she had broad shoulders that looked misshapen atop her slender figure. That was, however, set right by the deliberate lack of her make-up, whilst her auburn hair was scraped back into a loose bun upon her head. A hawkish nose lay prominent on her face and lingered cruelly over a mouth full of jagged teeth. Strangest of all was her raspy voice which had often sounded curt when she dealt with clients. The PR industry was an industry that required finesse and an amiable persona and, so far, she hadn't really conveyed any of those traits. How the hell had she landed, and more importantly kept, the job that she was in.

Friendship had developed over a discussion about her tuna sandwich. It was a cold, wet Wednesday afternoon and she had mentioned to him that she was looking forward to her days off. She didn't work Thursday's or Friday's, she explained. He already knew. The subject was already a contentious issue, and a negative talking point amongst the other members of staff. It had forged resentment that had made her the target of Chinese whispers and a passive-aggressive hate campaign. Rumours, as in most places of work, had long since become known facts. She had become the social pariah of the office, yet didn't seem to care that she had been blackballed from the outset.

Eventually when enough conversation had passed between them, and the spurious accusations had been dispelled, she finally asked him.

"Why don't you join the others for lunch? And why do you sit in here when you know how they all feel about me?" He was astounded. He hadn't assumed anything about her perception, or lack of, until that moment; but now that she mentioned it, it occurred to him that she was more astute than people might give her credit for. It made the treatment of her seem all the more cruel. He wondered if her being so insular was a mode of self-protection. He answered the question with another question.

"If you know how they feel about you, why do you do nothing to change it?" She shrugged and ran her fingers across the bend in her newspaper. A steaming hot mug sat between them, the scent of coffee beans masking the insidious whiff of the vent.

"Maybe, I don't care very much. I don't speak their language, and I don't tell them what they want to hear. Therefore, I must be a bitch". Her eyelids rose dismissively. Joe had always got on relatively well with most of his colleagues, but Louise wasn't the first person to speak of their bullish and mob mentality.

The in-crowd had already started to return from their lunch. High spirits resounded across the floor. Joe and Louise were laughing gently as they left the cafeteria, her face notably softened as she enjoyed the company of somebody other than her kindle or newspaper editor. '…….. Widow Cranky'. Joe hadn't heard the exact words from Barry Millar, but there was definitely an aura of cruelty in his tone; a note of sarcasm and spite.

"Barry, you're a moron. Get a life!", Joe snapped. Barry looked back at him, his bravado disappearing, and managed the hint of a scowl. Louise put her hand on his arm.

"Don't fight my battle, Joe. It's not worth it". She smiled gratefully though.

"It's worth it to me. He's a bully. You know you don't have to put up with it". She nudged her head to the side.

"The place is full of them. I can either suck it up or spend the rest of my working life fighting against it". She gave him a gentle tug on the arm and returned to her desk. Joe looked across the office at the herd of laughing sheep and felt himself rage as it became more obvious that she was the target of bullying. He wanted to march over and tell them exactly what he thought, but he knew better. Instead, he stared in and pondered to himself that something had to change.

2.

Over the days and weeks and months, friendship crept up on them, almost without warning. A chat over coffee during break time soon turned into lunches at Cote's Bar which then turned into quick drinks after work which then turned into regular conversations by telephone. It was her self-depreciation and her riotous laughter that was her real personality asset. She was able to poke fun at herself, and even acknowledged some of the wicked slurs that had been cast upon her by her continuously abrasive work mates. She spoke often, and with real affection, of her husband and their two children; Christina and Lauren. There had been a third baby in the set of triplets, but she had died little more than two hours into her life. Joe, in turn, spoke of his difficult relationship with his partner Brian. They had recently decided to live together after being in an on/off relationship for nearly ten years. Joe was struggling with elements of it, although became defensive when she suggested that he may have a commitment phobia. The more time Joe spent with Louise, the more others started to accept her. She even found herself being invited for lunch. The new relaxed attitude seemed to have a positive effect on her, and she became more relatable and easy to be around. Even Barry Millar eased up on the Widow Cranky jokes.

It was the Wednesday before the Easter Holiday when Louise asked, practically begged, Joe to accompany her to Cote's. When they arrived, she ordered a coffee for herself and a vodka tonic for him, before draping her suit jacket across the back of a thick oak chair.

"So, what's eating you?" he asked, immediately sensing her anxiety. What wasn't inflected in her voice was written across her face. Her pallor was slightly grey, and he wondered if she was becoming ill. She rubbed continuously at her arm, and looked as if she might fall out of the chair at any moment.

"I'm not feeling great, I have this bowel condition, and it's really playing up. Other than that I'm fine". She continued to fidget with her arm.

"So why didn't you go home, instead of coming to the pub", he asked sharply. Her eyes glistened as if tears were forming and about to flood her lids.

"What's wrong, Lou?" His voice lowered to a gravelly whisper, and he watched tears fall to her chin. The entire time that she sobbed, she never let go of her arm, and it was making Joe increasingly anxious. He barely recognised her now. The woman who sat before him was not the steely eyed motor mouth that he had come to know. Then she dabbed at her eyes, pulled back her shoulder and made a feeble attempt at composure.

"I don't want to talk about it", she finally offered, too breezily.

"So what the hell am I doing here?" he demanded, unable to conceal his irritation. She pulled the coffee mug to her lips and hid her face behind the steam for a moment. When she pulled it away, and the mist passed, she became the Louise who he knew again.

"I really don't want to talk about it, so let's just drop the subject." She rubbed her arm again. What the hell was going on with that, he wondered? He gently pulled it, and threw back the cuff of her jersey. She tried to snatch it away.

"What the hell?" Her wrist was blackened under the grip of somebody's hand, the subsequent bruise spreading up the inside of her forearm. He looked at her in shock.

"Lou, do you want to tell me what the hell is going on?"

3.

On the way to the bus stop, she said nothing. The silence was so eerie that they could hear the sound of heels click against the asphalt. He didn't push her on the subject. When he had pushed to hard, she had become emotional again. Her tears had come swift and thick after he had forced her to open up. She had talked so affectionately about her husband that Joe didn't know how it could possibly be his doing. Had she fallen maybe? Why, after months of opening up to each other, did she suddenly shut tighter than a clam? He wanted to ask her outright, but he knew better than to probe into somebody else's life. Finally when he spoke, it wasn't about the bruise on her arm, or her tears.

"Brian and I are off to Poland in September". She smiled half-heartedly, but didn't speak. "Cannot wait. Do you know when we were last away on holiday together? Three years!" he declared with evident displeasure. He carried on speaking when it was obvious that she wasn't in the mood for speaking. "We're staying in the old town, you know, Krakow. Maybe do the tour of the camps". She stopped at the bus stop and turned to face him.

"Adam and I would love to get away, but you know, it's difficult to take the girls out of school", she finally muttered. Joe nodded in acknowledgment. The bus came into the distance, and pulled up towards them as silence descended again. Finally, he saw her onto the bus and then started the fifteen minute stroll to his own house. For the entire journey, he could think of nothing else but Louise and her husband. How could somebody who seemed so steely and determined be the victim of domestic abuse? It didn't seem plausible that this could be happening to her, and yet she had remained so tight lipped about the cause of that massive bruise. There had been something quite deliberate in the way she had drawn attention to it and then completely avoided his questions. What was it she was trying to tell him? Or, more to the point, what was it that she was trying to conceal from him? Whatever was going on in that house, Joe was determined that he would get to the bottom of it. Whatever trouble his friend Louise was in; she would not be going through it alone.

4.

Joe called Louise later that night. He had arrived home to complete silence. The place was perfectly still. Brian was nowhere to be found.

"You okay?" She hesitated.

"I'm okay, honest. I'm sorry that I was a bit off today. I'm just a little worn out". Her breathing was laboured, as if she had been running, or fighting...

"Hey don't worry, we all have days like that. What are friends for, eh?" His voice was reassuring, soft with an East coast lilt, and it was one of the things that made her feel at ease around him.

"Not you, though, Mr Sunshine". The words had tumbled out of her mouth before she had even put her brain into first gear. Had she sounded rude, she wondered? She hadn't meant to. It was meant as a compliment; an acknowledgement of the friendship that he had shown her when nobody else had given her daylight.

"You think?" he asked, slightly amused. "You think I've not got insecurities? God, you need your contacts changed", he laughed then. A hearty, comforting laugh that told her not to be worried and that he hadn't been offended. "Look at me and Brian. Poor guy can't even go to the kitchen to take a call without me thinking he's arranging a secret affair. It took me years to agree to live with him because I thought he would break my heart, or find somebody better. So, don't think that I've not got my own shit going on, because I have. I just mask it well". She tutted emphatically.

"We're a right pair, eh?" He couldn't disagree with that.

"Anyway, I just wanted to check in. Make sure you're okay. I'll speak to you tomorrow probably". The phone call ended on a high and he was pleased to hear that she sounded a whole lot more upbeat than she had in the bar. Maybe he had over-reacted to the bruises. Maybe, as she had explained coming out of the bar, she had fallen and twisted it. He thought of another time where he had noticed a badly concealed black eye, and he genuinely wondered what the hell was going on in her house. He sat spooning microwavable meatballs and pasta around a half empty bowl, and continued to imagine the terrible cruelty that she must be enduring. He wished to god that there was something he could do for her.

5.

When Louise Bradshaw failed to show up for work on the Tuesday after Easter, Joe became panicked. For no other reason than the fact that he couldn't take the knowledge of that bruised arm out of his mind. Not only that, but her guarded reaction also gave him concern. Had she fallen, wouldn't she just say she had fallen? Mumbles about a falling out quickly grew arms and legs and crawled across the gossip corners of the office. Joe simply shrugged and returned his concern back to his missing friend. He sent her an SMS just after eleven thirty and eyed his phone repeatedly for a response. It didn't come. He then rapped on the door of his boss, Arthur, and peered across the desk.

"Was just wondering about Louise, I thought she was supposed to be in today?" Arthur barely lifted his eyes from the paperwork in front of him.

"Sick, I'm afraid! Not ideal, but I'm sure we'll manage". Joe returned to his desk and thought of calling her. Why was he so worried though? His boss telling him she was off sick should have alleviated his worry, but it only compounded it more. She'd obviously called in to work to let them know she was sick, so he had to accept that she wasn't coming in and pray to God that nothing bad had happened to her.

He continued to message Louise throughout the Wednesday, but still heard nothing in response. By the afternoon, his stomach had twisted in anxiety. He rang her phone, but she didn't answer. So he rang again. When she still didn't reply, he picked up the phone and dialled the number of Teresa Jordan in HR. He and Teresa had been friends for more than a hundred dog years, and once had the same friendship that he and Louise now enjoyed. They had been the new kids in the office more than ten years ago, and had probably suffered a similar welcome to the one that Louise had endured, but they quickly wore the clique's down when it became apparent that they didn't really care what everybody else thought.

"Hey Teresa, I need a favour". She feigned surprise.

"What, no hello? How you doing? Just 'I need a favour'". She lowered her voice to try and emulate his.

"That's a rubbish impersonation", he laughed loudly.

"What? Too butch? Okay, sweets, what's the favour?" A minute later he scribbled Louise's address on to his notepad, suddenly shocked that he didn't even know where she lived, and then carried out a five minute conversation with Teresa about their weekend past.   They'd catch up soon. Dinner and drinks and then a dozen more drinks.

6.

Brian had cooked that night when Joe returned home. Pre-occupied with the fact that Louise hadn't responded to any of his messages over the past two days, he was hell-bent on visiting her home as soon as he had changed. After all, she could be really sick. Or really hurt. Or maybe she was one of those people who just liked to be left alone and sweat it out. The fact that she hadn't replied to a single message really quite concerned him though. Brian was becoming infuriated. "If she wants you to know, she'll tell you" he had chanted over and over as if it were his new mantra. He was determined that he and Joe would enjoy a Louise Bradshaw-free evening, pull themselves out of her quagmire, and simply just enjoy the moment. He had cooked grilled chicken in a Chianti sauce with olives and parmesan cheese. He dimmed their lounge so that a triumvirate of candles flickered and emulated flames on the wall. A bottle of wine later and Joe felt just relaxed enough to allow Brian to lead him to the bedroom where Louise Bradshaw became just a distant thought.

7.

Just when he was about to approach Arthur Milligan about his concerns, Joe watched Louise burst through the security door of the office. She looked ghastly. Her eyes were sunken inside the black rims of her reading glasses. She had attempted to mask the greying pastiness with a dab of foundation, but it wasn't really concealing anything. It was Thursday morning, and she wasn't due to work until the following Monday.

"You look awful, why are you even here?" Her eyes darted from Arthur's door to meet with his.

"I didn't follow the sickness absence procedure, so I have to make up my days or lose pay", she replied, tautly.

"Can they do that?" She shrugged. She didn't know, but she didn't have the urge to fight it.

"I had to go to accident and emergency on Monday night", she finally explained. Lines furrowed across his forehead as he looked increasingly worried for her.

"Why?"

"I had a flare up of IBS, stomach cramps, felt sick; they think it might be a problem with my gall bladder". He didn't recall her ever talking about having any bowel condition. A doubt lingered between the two, almost like an invisible question mark. "Doctor thinks it might have to come out".

"That's awful" he conceded and watched as she tucked herself behind her desk and spent the morning looking dismal. Something niggled at the back of his mind, but he could not find the words to express it.

Later on that day as they sat in the dim light of the kitchen, Louise stroked at her arm and ran her eyes across the newspaper. The arm stroking wasn't lost on Joe who still wanted answers. Their eyes met suddenly and he was sure he saw a flash of guilt spread across her flushing face.

"Louise, if you need my help, you only need to ask", he finally offered, and didn't even try to hide away his worry. She nodded her head.

"I know, but I'm fine. Other than a throbbing stomach, I'm honestly fine". His lips rose in a sympathetic half-smile.

"Louise, I know it's not my business and I don't want to offend you, but I really have to ask you this. God, how do I say it? Does your husband beat you?" He finally asked the question that had sat between them previously in Cote's and now over lunch. She looked shocked, like he had struck her. Her eyes narrowed now, angrily.

"No!" she snapped, her voice rising slightly. Denial! "No, he does not. And how dare you imply it". Her voice calmed slightly and she returned to the woman he had first met all those months ago in the bleak winter; grimacing and brisk.

"I'm s-sorry", he stuttered, suddenly embarrassed that he had pushed too hard and evidently stepped over the line.

"Well you bloody should be. How could you even think that. I told you that I had fallen. I told you I've been sick." He continued to apologise profusely, and she softened then, seeing the awkward and apologetic expression on his face "I'm just really tired and sore. I couldn't take anything for the pain this morning or I'd be dead on my feet". Joe's face was still a boiling shade of puce long after she had shuffled out of the kitchen. She had protested too hard though. If there was one thing he was now certain of, it was that she was most definitely in some kind of trouble. All it would take now was for him to prove it.

8.

"I really want to go and smack his teeth out". Joe had been ranting about Adam Bradshaw for fifteen minutes. Brian sighed unsympathetically. Truthfully, he didn't care much for Louise. She had been rude and lofty on the previous occasions he had met her, and he didn't really understand the dynamic of the friendship between her and Joe. He was amused by Joe's tantrum though. He longed for him to be this passionate about their troubles and would give his right arm to hear him fight for their relationship in the same way.

"It's not our business, Joe" he said as he pointed his fork across the table. There was still something that bothered Joe though as he thought about how she would talk about Adam in such high esteem. It hadn't added up when his thoughts turned to this violent man. The two just didn't equate. Had it only recently transpired? It was the only thing that made sense. When he considered how candid and outspoken she could be, and how Adam had seemed to be the best thing in her life, it really made him wonder about what had really been going on. He had seen that violent bruise on her arm though, she had attempted to mask a quite visible bruising around her eye on a previous occasion, and her erratic behaviour and attendance at work had really raised questions.

The absences from work became more frequent, and Joe became more concerned for Louise's safety. The final straw for Joe, and possibly Brian, was when she turned up to their home in tears. There was a tiny bruise on her forehead and Joe could have pre-empted her excuse before it even tumbled off her tongue. She had walked into the door. The door was at an odd angle. Maybe she had banged it when she had fallen to the floor. 'Maybe she had walked into Adam's fist and she should stop covering', although Joe knew better than to say it. The dishevelled look and the tinge of wine from her breath rang alarm bells for Brian, but Joe could only defend her and say it was no surprise to anybody that she looked worse for wear after what she had had to endure. Brian daren't argue. After he stormed to bed, feigning a headache, Joe finally broached the subject.

"We can help you get yourself and your girls away from him".

"I don't want to leave", she had offered with little in the way of her usual feisty retort.

"But he hurts you Lou, and what about when you're gone, and he moves onto your girls".

"He won't do that. He just loses his temper. He's busy at work, under stress, and I struggle to keep on top of the house. He only wants a wife who manages to keep the house clean and get the girls to bed on time". Her defence tumbled out into the air and Joe was shocked that she even believed what she was saying. It almost sounded as if she were excusing his behaviour and blaming herself. Joe felt sick.

9.

Louise must have crept out in the middle of the night when Joe and Brian were sleeping. The duvet was folded and quartered and placed at the end of the sofa. There was no note, no other indication that she had ever been there. It was no shock to him when he arrived at work with two minutes to spare, and she was nowhere to be found. He had thought of her when he woke to the squawk of his alarm. He had thought of her when he was in the shower, where he had become so reviled that he almost bellowed his anger into the steaming air. He had thought of her during most of his twenty minute walk to work where the calmer voice in his mind fought against the furious rant of his other voice, and they had drowned out the sound of his favourite Eurythmics songs. Now, he stared at her empty desk and then drew his eyes across the room at all the oblivious onlookers who had contributed to the misery of this unhappy and abused woman. He raged within himself and wanted to storm through the office, wail like a hurricane, and pour the truth all over them. Instead, he decided he was going to her house. This time, nothing would stop him.

10.

"Arthur, I need to take a half day. I've felt lousy all night and managed to get an appointment with my GP". Arthur waved nonchalantly whilst barely lifting his eyes from the sports page of an internet website. Tea break passed and Joe still couldn't shake Louise from his head. He thought of their conversation from the night before. They had talked until one in the morning, and it showed on his face. Perhaps that's why Arthur hadn't even questioned his decision to leave at lunch time. Perhaps he looked exactly as worn as he felt. His blonde hair was tousled on top of his head so that it revealed the line of his forehead. His light blue eyes, the colour of a naked sky on a summer day, glinted with tears of tiredness. His muscles ached, as if they hadn't quite come to life after a restless night of Brian's snoring amidst vivid dreams of Louise running from a man who he didn't recognise. He was still anxious that she had crept away in the night without leaving a note or messaging him.

He closed his PC down just after 12 noon and made his way to the bus stop. He dropped a two pound coin into the old bus bank and made the thirty minute journey across town to Louise's address. His hands shook as he arrived at the corner of the street where she lived. What if Adam Bradshaw hadn't gone to work today? What if Louise's disappearing routine the night before had made things worse? What if his arrival at her house wasn't a welcome intervention, but an invite for her husband to dole out his own brand of punishment? As he moved towards the secure entry panel at the front of their flat, he punched in the numbers; *two, one, call*. The buzzer screamed to life. A knot loosened in his stomach. Finally, a man's voice boomed from the intercom.

"Hello".

"Erm, hello, is Louise there?" Silence. "Hello, is Louise home?" Still nothing.

"Is this some kind of joke?" the voice crackled into the intercom. Joe didn't understand.

"This is Louise's friend Joe. From work. I'm here to see her". The buzzer clicked off. Joe sighed angrily. He was about to punch the buttons in again when Adam Bradshaw emerged from the tail of the stairs. He threw open the secure door, fury blazoned across his face, and pointed angrily at Joe. The words didn't come immediately. His face reddened.

"If you don't get away from my property, I'm calling the police".

"Call the police?" Joe felt his nerve shift and a tingle flushed his face. "Go ahead; I'm sure they'd love to know what you do to your wife".

Joe didn't know it was possible for a man to look angrier, but Adam just about toppled down the last few stairs as he shoved at Joe.

"What I do to my wife? I can't do anything to my wife, you sicko. She's dead!"

11.

Joe felt as if he had been sucker punched in the stomach. He wanted to check for the bruising. He kept hearing the words echo through his mind as he strolled home. "Dead! Dead! Dead!" Over and over again. There was an empty brightness spread across the sky and the sun blazed down onto the pavement. Adam Bradshaw had stormed back into the house without explanation and Joe had been left shocked on the street as he tried to piece together what had happened from the moment Louise had left their house in the middle of the night and the moment she arrived home to her feral husband. There had been nothing to suggest anything violent had taken place at their house. No blockade, no police, no tears from Adam. Just an angry man who was either a very good actor or telling the truth. None of this made sense to Joe. What was he missing? As he unlocked his front door, and tumbled into the hallway, he could hear Brian's voice boom from the lounge before he had even left the hallway. He listened to hear if Brian was angry or excited. He couldn't tell at first. Was he on the phone? As Joe entered their lounge, he saw Brian wave animatedly. He lowered his arms as he walked over to embrace Joe. He shook his head in irritation as they hugged. Joe looked towards the woman who sat on the sofa with her back to him. She turned around, and he gasped! "Louise?"

12.

Brian watched the spectacle of emotion as if he were witnessing a Shakespeare performance. His mouth was agape in shock and he couldn't believe that Joe was buying any of this. His dislike for Louise had intensified so much that he wondered if he were merely jealous. It wasn't that, though. She was purely and simply the most manipulative woman he had ever met. He wondered if her husband had beaten her at all, yet the physical evidence suggested it most definitely did happen. He couldn't put his finger on it, but he didn't trust her a bit. She didn't strike him as the type of woman who would allow a man to hit her, and he had said as much right before Joe had walked through the door. It hadn't been received well by her at all. He was on the cusp of throwing her out of his flat when Joe sailed through the door. 'Damn it, when is this woman going to get out of our life', he thought to himself.

"Why the hell would Adam tell me you were dead?" Joe demanded, as Brian's eyes widened.

"He said what?" A myriad of confusion, frustration and irritation passed through the room. Brian saw the panic flicker across her face. It almost amused him. She was searching her bank of excuses for something plausible.

"He said I'm dead to him", she finally offered. Brian rolled his eyes so far back into his head that his pupils almost disappeared. "He thinks I'm having it off with you. That we've been having an affair since we started befriending each other. I told him that it was absolute rubbish, but he just won't be told". Joe's eyes tightened.

"Oh for gawd sake!" Brian couldn't believe what he was hearing. He didn't believe a word of it.

"You're not letting this idiot tell you that her husband thinks she's having an affair with a bloody gay man?"

"Brian, just…" Joe lifted his hand midway through the sentence and watched as Brian sunk into the chair. "So, he thinks that you and I are having a secret affair. Why? WHY?" It made sense now why Adam might be so hostile towards him, but how sick would a person have to be to claim that his wife was dead when she was very much alive. Adam Bradshaw was so convincing though. What the hell had gone on between them to make Adam so angry that he would beat her and then declare her to be dead.

13.

"So, what the hell are we going to do?" Joe demanded irritably. Brian looked up in horror.

"WE? What are WE going to do? WE are going to stay the hell out of it and let those psycho's sort out their own ugly mess". He pointed accusingly at Louise, and she began to sob loudly. Any minute now, she might climb into the vortex of her own life and be swallowed up whole. Joe moved in towards her and threw his arms around her shoulder. She flinched. If Brian hadn't felt so disgusted, he might have admired her flawless performance. He wanted to applaud her. He wanted to stand up and scream "Bravo!" However, the disgust moved around his mouth so vividly that it almost dehydrated him. When he could take no more, he simply got up and left. He snatched Joe's jacket on his way out the door. Joe sighed. He felt torn. He wanted to support Brian, but he felt compelled by this woman's trouble. He wanted to save her from a man who could humiliate and beat her and then throw her out of her own children's lives. He sat there on the sofa and watched her wring every tear out of the sodden napkin she held between her fingers.

"Wine?" he finally asked, and passed her the box of wipes from the table. "Here, we'll need to get something to soften those eyes". She thanked him and rested back against the sofa arm, whilst he disappeared into the kitchen.

14.

Adam Bradshaw was broader than he looked in his picture. To Brian's eyes, his face was hardened by the knowledge that he had beaten his wife. In other circumstances, the man would have been quite striking. The parting in his hair probably aged him somewhat, as did the choice of attire. As he threw open the security door, wearing an un-cuffed sky blue shirt and navy trousers, his eyes bore straight into Brian and he looked away nervously.

Brian had found Louise's address in Joe's jacket pocket. It hadn't been a conscious decision to come here and confront Adam, and now that he was here, he was already regretting it. He felt as if he were crawling across the bones of somebody else's life. It felt ugly and intrusive and he wanted to climb back down the stairs and get back in his car and make the 3 minute drive back to his own house. Was it so difficult for him to stand up for himself? Or for Joe, who he knew was being taken for a mug.

"I'm here about your wife". Adam recoiled.

"She's a popular subject today", he said, notably calmer than he had been when Joe had buzzed him.

"It seems so. Joe, the man who came to see you earlier, is my partner". Adam simply shrugged. "Your wife is at my house right now, claiming that you think my partner is having an affair with her. Which is, quite frankly, ridiculous as you can probably now imagine". Brian's voice was measured, unprovocative and slightly shaky from his rising nerves.

"I'm sorry! My wife has said that I think she's having an affair?" He looked incredulous, as if somebody had just told him the sky was falling in. "And when did she say this?" Brian felt his bowels shift. It was becoming clear to him that he wasn't playing with all the facts.

"Today! Just now!" Adam suddenly laughed; a sarcastic belittling laugh that made Brian feel slightly stupid and he wished that he hadn't come at all.

"Are you and your friend, Joe was it?"

"He's my partner, actually", Brian said quietly, pointlessly.

" Are you on something?" Brian shook his head.

"No. I think we have a problem though. If I'm being truthful, Mr Bradshaw, I just really want your wife out of my house". Adam's fist clenched.

"I don't know how many other ways to say this. To you, and your...partner", he looked almost tearful. "So I'll say it one more time. I'll say it for your benefit", his teeth clenched then "I'll say it for your partner's benefit and for anybody else who is in any double, my wife Louise...IS...DEAD!" Brian didn't understand.

"She said you would say that, that she was dead to you because you were so angry", he spoke persuasively. Adam's eyes didn't move. They simply bore through Brian as if he were invisible.

"She can't tell you anything, BECAUSE...SHE'S...DEEEAD!!! I don't know who you've got sitting on your sofa, but my wife died six months ago".

15.

Joe eyed her through the crack in the kitchen door as she wrestled with her bag for her mobile phone. He watched her send an SMS. There was ferocity to her movement that caught his breath. Her behaviour seemed to change. She was no longer shrunken, or desolate. She punched the buttons of her phone quickly. He saw her rest onto the back of the sofa. The look on her face, calculating and hostile, disturbed him so deeply that he couldn't believe she was the same woman. He watched as she pinched the skin on her arm and twisted it around her index finger and her thumb. It would go red soon. Then it would most likely bruise. Then she pulled up her V-neck and dragged her finger nails down the right hand of her stomach. She was hurting herself. It wasn't her husband. It wasn't some mystery illness. It was just Louise Bradshaw herself. She was hurting herself and letting him believe that it was her husband who was beating her. Joe felt more horrified than he had ever been in his life.

Brian looked at the photo of the pretty blonde woman crammed between her gregarious daughters.

"I don't know what to say, I'm stumped". Louise Bradshaw was certainly not the woman who he had come to know over the past months, and Adam Bradshaw's behaviour was not the behaviour of the man he had been told about.

"Me neither, but you seem to have been the victim of a ridiculous joke". He looked less concerned now. Like it was Brian and Joe's problem, instead of his own. Somebody had taken his wife's identity and he didn't seem to care.

"Aren't you furious?" Adam shook his head.

"I don't have the energy to be furious. Besides, I only have your word that this woman even exists? What if you and your partner are off your rockers yourselves?" Brian laughed.
"Oh, she's real. She's sat on my sofa right now and pretending that you have beaten her".

"And she told you that it was me?" Actually, Brian realised, she had never said he was beating her.

"Uhm, no, she didn't say it." Adam sighed loudly. This *game* was becoming tiresome.

"So, this woman, who I don't even know, says she's my dead wife? Then, you two jokesters turn up here, accusing me of beating my invisible dead wife? Even though my dead wife, who is in your house right now, hasn't actually said that I'm beating her? Are you really serious? This is how you want to play this?" He was livid now.

"She's in our house, claiming she's your wife, and IMPLYING that you have hurt her. She has bruises and has turned up several times in tears". Brian's eyes moved back to the photo of the woman and her two daughters. A triumvirate of pictures were spread behind them. Mostly of the twins. They looked so much like their mother; the woman in the photo. Then, Brian gasped as Adam's voice trailed off. The last picture was of two women and a set of twins. Louise Bradshaw smiled from ear to ear, whilst the twins appeared to tease each other. The final woman staring back at him was the mystery woman that would now be sitting on his sofa and spindling her web of lies.

17.

Joe nervously rinsed cold water through the glass and saw the droplets shimmer. She hadn't uttered a word in five minutes. The wine was uncorked and ready to pour, but he was dragging the process out for as long as he could. He couldn't hide in the kitchen for much longer. Should he call the police? Where was his phone?

"Crap!" The realisation spread across him. His phone was in his jacket pocket, which Brian was now wearing.

"Need a hand?" she called. He shuddered.

"No, no, just be a minute". Had she heard the quiver in his voice? Could she smell the fear which was now so palpable that he could smell it himself. He carried two wet glasses and the bottle slowly into the lounge and watched her rub her arm back and forth. He poured a little of the oaky red into the glass and watched as it's legs crawled up the glass quickly. He didn't pour the second glass. His hands were shaking. He put the bottle onto the table at the end of the sofa. As he looked back at her, she pulled her hand away and revealed her work of art. It hadn't quite reddened yet. She looked disappointed. He handed her the poured glass.

"Doesn't quite work on demand, does it?" She looked up. If he was expecting shock, he would be disappointed. He pondered over her reaction. Anger? Sadness? Relief? He couldn't be sure.
"I saw you watching me", she announced, her mask of cordiality dropping in favour of the hawk-like ferocity that had made her so unpopular with her other colleagues. "You've probably guessed. My husband doesn't hit me. My husband barely knows I'm alive, actually." She necked half the contents of the glass. He felt ridiculous now, standing here in front of her waiting on her every word, and not able to predict what her next move would be. She looked ugly though.   Finally, he sat on the armchair and faced her. She cackled. A witch-like shriek breaking through the still.

"Why did you want us all to think your husband was beating you?" She looked unfazed. It unsettled him.

"You're too stupid to understand", she answered dismissively. He felt humiliated. Like he had been duped by somebody much cleverer than himself. He wasn't alone. She did feel clever. She felt downright triumphant because something had finally been about her.

"Try me!"

"Okay. I live an empty life. My girls are obsessed with each other. My husband works so much. Work mates treat me like they've wiped me from their show, and the few friends that Adam allowed me to have now find ways of avoiding me". She looked at him for a reaction.

"Lies. LIES. More lies. You actually believe what you're saying, don't you". She laughed, maliciously. He wondered just how much she was enjoying this.

"Not lies! Slight embellishments perhaps".

"I want you out. You miserable evil bitch!" His voice had gone deeper now, a cry of defiance. She wore a look of mock surprise and stood up. She threw back the remnants of her wine glass and threw it on the sofa. He stood up and leaned towards her, two faces of angry insolence meeting for the first time, and spoke once more to her. "Don't ever come back here, Louise, or…" An angry voice interrupted him before he was able to finish the threat.

"Don't call her Louise."

18.

"So why the hell did you do it, Debra?" Adam stepped out of the doorframe and saw her move angrily towards him.

"Debra? Who the hell is Debra?" Joe asked, his voice still swirling in his buiilding adrenalin. He followed Adam's puzzled gaze.

"My wife's sister", he answered flatly, his words dripping with finality. Joe tried to pull his thoughts together, but they were splitting and spinning through his mind, clashing like feral beasts in the wilderness. The tension rose in the room as the woman, Debra, reached for the bottle of red wine on the table.

"That won't do you any good, Debra. I've called the police on my way over here". Her face changed then. She looked betrayed. Joe's eyes darted from her to Adam, and then to Brian and wondered how the two men had come to be together. The time for questions would be later though. The next few moments blurred as Debra sidled up to Adam, clutching the bottle ferociously. A feast of feral rage lay out before them.

"Your wife's sister?" she demanded. "IS THAT ALL I AM TO YOU?" Her voice rose, and she began to scream like a scalded cat. Adam stood back, edging away from her. Brian and Joe both looked on in horror.

"Why did you do it?" he demanded again.

"You really want to know", she hissed. He shook his head. "You never noticed me. That's why. I did everything I could for you after Louise died and I might as well have been invisible". His eyes creased in disbelief. "I wanted so much to be part of your life, and you didn't even notice me". Adam couldn't believe what he was hearing. He sniffed at her, but he didn't give her the benefit of his disgust, because that would have been more than she deserved from him.

"You never change, Debra. If you could have had Louise's life years ago, you would have taken it all, wouldn't you?" Joe could hear her teeth grit. "That's why she cut down on your time with the girls, you know, and saw less of you". She snarled now. "She sensed your jealousy. You were so jealous that you could hardly breathe". He tutted sarcastically. "Jealous of your own sister. What kind of person wants to take over their dead sister's life?" She moved around the side of Adam so that she had placed herself in the middle of him and Brian.

"She was so perfect, my sister, wasn't she? Irreplaceable? That's what you said. Clearly not, though Adam. Do you know how easy it was just to step into her life. Poor, dreary little Louise". Joe couldn't believe a person would be so vile about their own sister. Who was this woman who had infiltrated his life and made him believe that she was a good person; a victim even. "I could have taken everything and you wouldn't even have noticed, Adam". She moved towards him again so that he could feel her breath on his neck. He felt violated. Joe saw it happen before he was able to move a muscle. It happened so quickly that none of them saw it coming until her arm was hurtling through the air. She lifted the bottle above Adam's head and brought it crashing down.

19.

Blood spurted from his shattered vein as glass crashed around him.

20.

Joe watched in terror as Brian grabbed her wrist and pulled the bottle away from Adam. She was stronger than he had thought. Her broad shoulders gave her an upper strength that might have been deceiving against the rest of her frame. Quicker than lightning, she spun round and screamed. A surging throttle of a scream that echoed through the atmosphere.

"Brian! No!" Joe tried to move, but felt himself frozen in place. He could only watch it unfold before him. The bottle now landed on the side of Brian's head. Blood spurted from a vein in his forehead. He lost his grip on her wrist and fell to the floor. Adam had thrown himself out of harm's way and landed on the floor. Joe rushed towards her and grabbed for her wrist before she could inflict any more damage with the bottle. Outside, sirens wailed. They really had called the police. She was about to bring the remnants of the bottle down on Brian's head again when Joe threw himself against her and knocked her to the floor. Her arms flailed as the bottle fell from her hand. Fragments of glass lay all around her. She wriggled violently as Joe landed on top of her. She screamed again, this time piercing the tunnel of his ears. Brian stirred a few yards away and reached for his cut head. Joe grabbed for her face angrily. He wanted to kill her for what she had done to them, but he wanted her to realise what she done more. She grabbed for his throat, but missed by an inch. She looked frenzied as he wrapped a strand of her hair in his hand and knocked her head against the floor. Once, twice, three times. She felt the thud at the back of her head. Her world went out of focus then. Everything spun for a few moments before it began to fade. The room disappeared. The sirens had stopped.

21.

Debra found herself staring at two police officers and the three men who she had just attacked. She stared at ten murderous eyes, and went frigid with fear. "Please don't kill me, please don't kill me", she cried, repeatedly. She had only wanted to be loved by Adam and her sister's two daughters. She hadn't stolen Louise's life. She had honoured it. As the police officer's gently reached down and helped her onto her knees, her sobbing whine rose to a howl. Debra Williams was still shrieking when she was dragged out of Joe and Brian's lounge and onto the street. Tears lay heavy on her cheek. She was babbling something inaudible as she was pulled past Adam, Brian and Joe. She disappeared from sight as she was pushed into the back seat of the police car, and then as the police car pulled away from the front of the house, Brian felt a pang of joy rattle within. Adam Bradshaw shook their hand and thanked them for bringing her lie to his attention, but he never seemed fully perturbed by the revelation that his former sister-in-law had not only stole his wife's identity, but that she had attempted to frame him for abusing her. Joe and Brian wouldn't really know if he had refused her advances, or if he was even aware that any of her deceit had transpired. Joe thought of the "Widow Cranky" slur that had been attached to her by their colleagues and he would later find out that most of them had already discovered the truth behind many of her lies. He was late to the table. Was he the only person who HADN'T known. He touched Brian's face where the blood dried around the line of his cheeks. He was thankful that Brian hadn't been badly hurt. He was also thankful that Louise, or Debra, would now be getting the help that she so desperately needed. He and Brian walked back towards the house as the sun drooped below the skyline. As they entered the house, Joe looked back and saw the blue and red lights flash in the distance. He wanted to smile then. A huge beaming smile of relief. He resisted the urge. Then he closed the door on Louise Bradshaw. Forever!

A SAMPLE OF "LOST GIRL" – COMING SOON

Flames crackled up the walls before licking at the edges of the ceiling. The fire had already burned through everything that was flammable in the room and now flared towards the door. Any minute now, the glass would break in the corroding heat and the fire would spread through the building. For now, it was contained to the reception area. As the window panes shattered in its unbridled rage, the cold breeze fanned the inferno and carried it out into the night air. The leather chairs and the wooden desk had already blackened, transformed to charcoal that would eventually smoulder on the floor. The hue of smoke billowed up as the skyline seethed in its wake. Meanwhile, the flames had finally spread into a store room that held copious amounts of flammable liquids, ensuring that the entire block would be scorched and reduced to ashes...

"I want to know what the hell you plan to do about the scum living in my block. I've got three addicts up my close. Last week they were stabbing each other on the landing. We're all sick of it". Peter felt his shoulders sag, and he desperately wanted a drink. Moreover, he wanted to crawl into a nearby drain and disappear. It was the exact reason he hated addressing at local level. They didn't understand the real agendas, or the long scope that he was aiming for. He cleared his throat and smiled awkwardly, rubbing his hand across his stubble...

As he fused with the crowd of bar flies who moved from one end of the centre to the other, he felt the need to acquire a drink himself. When he finally discovered where she was, after months of trying to find her, it had sent him into a spin. The myriad of emotions he had felt upon finding her and then coming face to face with her, even for just a fleeting moment, had exhausted him. Then another realisation came to him as he stopped outside his final stop of the day; he would make her pay.